Noted
6/99
NKc

Little Chicken

STORY BY Margaret Wise Brown

PICTURES BY Leonard Weisgard

HARPER & ROW, PUBLISHERS

Little Chicken
Copyright, 1943, by Harper & Row, Publishers, Incorporated
Text copyright renewed 1971 by Roberta Brown Rauch
Illustrations copyright renewed 1971 by Harper & Row, Publishers, Inc.
All rights reserved. No part of this book may be used or
reproduced in any manner whatsoever without written permission
except in the case of brief quotations embodied in critical
articles and reviews. Printed in the United States of America.
For information address Harper & Row, Publishers, Inc.,
10 East 53rd Street, New York, N.Y. 10022. Published simultaneously
in Canada by Fitzhenry & Whiteside Limited, Toronto.

Library of Congress Catalog Card Number: 43-16942
Trade ISBN 0-06-020739-6
Harpercrest ISBN 0-06-020740-X

LITTLE CHICKEN

Once there was a little chicken

who belonged to a Rabbit.
The Rabbit found him one day just
breaking out of an egg,
so he belonged to the Rabbit.

And he went where the Rabbit went.
When the Rabbit went for a walk,
the little chicken went for a walk.

When the Rabbit went into his hole to sleep
the little chicken went with him,
and curled up in the Rabbit's warm white fur.

When the Rabbit
ate big wet cabbages the little chicken drank a drop
of water from a wet cabbage leaf. The little chicken
didn't eat cabbages. Cabbages are too big.

He liked bugs and worms.
Worms and bugs and bugs and worms,—and seeds.
He went hopping about after them,
and when he caught them he ate them up.

Then one day the Rabbit wanted to run—
the way Rabbits run, on and on, for miles and miles.
So he said to the little chicken,
"Hop along and find someone to play with while I
go running around.
But don't forget to come home to me
before the sun goes down."
At first the little chicken was shy
"Who wants to play with a little chicken?" he said.
"Besides, I don't know anyone but you."
"Plenty of creatures want to play with a little chicken,"
said the Rabbit.
And he kicked up his hind legs and off he ran
over the hill.

There was the little chicken
alone in a very big world.

Along came flying a lady bug.

Would a lady bug want to play with a little chicken?

No indeed! Chickens eat bugs.

Then creepy crawly creepy crawly along came a furry fat caterpillar.
Would a furry fat caterpillar want to play with a little chicken?
No indeed! Chickens eat caterpillars.

Along came five fat sparrows.
Would they want to play with a little chicken?
Yes, they did. They were all birds.

Then came a little beaver,

A very little beaver who had just built a dam.

Would he want to play with a little chicken?

Not very much. He only liked to play with water and with

streams and dams.

The little chicken marched down the road till he came to a daisy field. He stopped to look at a daisy, a white one. He was getting a little lonesome. Then softly flutter flutter flitter flutter, along came a big pink butterfly with a black nose.

Would a big pink butterfly with a black nose want to play with a little chicken?

No!

The butterfly only played with flowers and with things up in the air.

The little chicken was sitting
in the dust of the road
watching a shadow,
when down the road, slowly,
came a tired old
workman.
Would a tired old workman want to play with a little
chicken?
Of course he would.

And then what do you think came along?
A great big round animal covered
with long sharp prickle quills.
        What could it be?
A porcupine—
But the little chicken didn't want to play with him.
He was too prickly.

Then came a grizzly bear.

    WOOF!

Would he want to play with a little chicken?

Not in this world.

Along came a silly little duck
Would a silly little duck want to play
with a little chicken?
They were just the same size,
the little duck and the little chicken.
But the chicken couldn't swim.

Along came a gentle little monkey
Would he want to play with a little chicken?
Of course he would. He was full
of monkey shines.
And he played with the
little chicken all afternoon.

But the little chicken had not forgotten what the Rabbit
had said.
And just as the sun went down, he hopped on home
to the Rabbit.
And the Rabbit ran home to the little chicken.
"Did you meet anyone who wanted to play with a little
chicken?" asked the Rabbit.
"Some who did and some who didn't,"
said the little chicken.

And he curled up in the Rabbit's warm white fur
and dreamed a little chicken dream.